OR
Echo

TIMBERWOLF Rivals

Sigmund Brouwer

illustrated by Graham Ross

ORCA BOOK PUBLISHERS

Library and Archives Canada Cataloguing in Publication

Brouwer, Sigmund, 1959-
Timberwolf rivals / Sigmund Brouwer ; illustrated by Graham Ross.

(Howling Timber Wolves)
(Orca echoes)
ISBN 978-1-55469-107-4

I. Ross, Graham, 1962- II. Title. III. Series.
IV. Series: Orca echoes
PS8553.R68467T5473 2009   JC813'.54   C2009-904580-X

First published in the United States, 2009
Library of Congress Control Number: 2009932872

Summary: In this seventh book in the Timberwolves series,
Johnny Maverick and his friends Tom and Stu pull more pranks on each other
in an attempt to win the prizes at the Valentine's Day dance contest.

Orca Book Publishers gratefully acknowledges the support for its publishing programs
provided by the following agencies: the Government of Canada through the Canada Book
Fund and the Canada Council for the Arts, and the Province of British Columbia
through the BC Arts Council and the Book Publishing Tax Credit.

Typesetting by Teresa Bubela
Cover artwork and interior illustrations by Graham Ross
Author photo by Bill Bilsley

ORCA BOOK PUBLISHERS
PO Box 5626, Stn. B
Victoria, BC Canada
V8R 6S4

ORCA BOOK PUBLISHERS
PO Box 468
Custer, WA USA
98240-0468

www.orcabook.com
Printed and bound in Canada.
Printed on 100% PCW recycled paper.

13 12 11 10 • 5 4 3 2

Chapter One
The New Girl

by Hunter

"Look," Tom Morgan said to his friends Johnny Maverick and Stu Duncan. All three boys played for the Howling Timberwolves hockey team. "There's the new girl."

It was a cold winter day. The boys stood near the flagpole on the school playground at recess.

"I hear she's a good dancer," Johnny said.

Stu didn't say anything. He was eating a sandwich with his mitts on. He ate a lot of sandwiches, with and without his mitts on.

"You think she's cute," Tom said.

"Do not," Johnny said. "No way! Yuck. Girls."

The new girl's name was Connie. She couldn't hear the boys talking, but she saw them looking at her. She smiled. It was a very friendly smile.

Johnny's face turned red when she smiled at them. He kicked some snow.

"She's a good dancer," Johnny said. "And the Howling Timberwolves fundraiser is next week."

"Do you mean the Valentine's Day dance contest?" Tom asked.

"Yes. I want to win the grand prize," Johnny said. "Even if it means going to a dance with a girl. The grand prize is a graphite hockey stick. Plus ten free dinners at the restaurant, and a bunch of other stuff too."

Johnny didn't have to explain which restaurant. The town of Howling was small. It only had one restaurant.

"Free dinners?" Stu asked. "*Ten* free dinners? *Ten*?"

"Every business in town has donated something toward the grand prize," Johnny explained.

3

"It's mostly parents that enter the dance contest. But I bet if someone danced with Connie, they would win."

"*Ten* free dinners?" Stu said again.

Connie still couldn't hear them talking. But she smiled at them again.

That's when Tom began to climb the flagpole. A rope ran up to the flag at the top. Tom pulled himself up the pole with the rope.

"What are you doing?" Johnny asked.

"I need Connie to be my dance partner," Tom said. He was almost halfway up the flagpole. "I'm an athlete. I know how to get a girl's attention."

He kept climbing.

It wasn't long before the students on the playground stopped what they were doing. Everybody gathered around the flagpole. Connie was there too.

Tom reached the top of the flagpole. He held on to the metal ball at the top with one hand. He looked down and grinned at Connie and waved.

She smiled back at him.

Everyone clapped. She did too.

The bell rang and recess ended. The students began to walk toward the school.

"Wait for me!" Tom yelled. The students stopped and turned to look back up at him.

Tom slid down the flagpole as fast as he could. He forgot about the part of the flagpole, near the bottom, where the rope wrapped around a metal cleat. The cleat stuck out on one side of the flagpole.

Tom smacked into the cleat at full speed.

All boys know hitting something like that, especially while sliding down a pole, is not good.

Tom's eyes opened wide. His face looked like a balloon that was losing air fast. He fell off the flagpole, curled into a ball and groaned.

"Wow," Johnny said to Stu, "he really does know how to get a girl's attention."

Chapter Two
The Tea Potty

"Thanks for coming with me," Eldridge said to Johnny and Stu.

Eldridge played on the Howling Timberwolves hockey team with Johnny and Stu. After school, the boys walked to Connie's house together.

"Connie asked me to help her with her computer," said Eldridge, "but I'm too shy to go to her house by myself."

"No problem," Johnny said to Eldridge. "We have plenty of time before our hockey game tonight. Besides, I'm your friend. I'm glad to help."

"That's not quite true," Stu told Eldridge. "Johnny's here because he wants Connie to be his dance partner at the Valentine's fundraiser."

"That's a good idea," Eldridge said. "I hear she's a great dancer. A person could win the contest with her as their partner. But I'm too shy to ask her."

"I just want to win the grand prize," Johnny said.

"I wonder if she has any cookies at her house," Stu said.

When they arrived at Connie's house, Johnny rang the doorbell.

Connie answered the door and smiled. Johnny's face turned red.

"Hello," Eldridge said. "We're here to help you with your computer."

"Hello," Stu said. "Do you have any cookies?"

Johnny was too busy being red in the face to say anything.

"Come in," Connie said. "My little sister Suzie is here too. She's only four years old."

Connie's house had a big living room. The computer was at a desk in one corner. The television was in another corner. Johnny and Stu sat on the

couch in front of the television. They used the remote control to find a hockey game. Eldridge went straight to work on the computer. Connie stood beside him and watched the computer screen.

"It would be nice to have some cookies," Stu said.

A little girl walked up to them, carrying a tray with a toy tea set on it.

"Cookies?" Stu asked.

"Pretend tea," Suzie said. "Would you like to have a tea party with my dolls?"

"Just dolls?" Stu asked. "No cookies?"

"I would love a tea party," Johnny told Suzie. Johnny whispered to Stu, "This is how to get a girl's attention. Not by climbing a flagpole but by being nice to her little sister."

Suzie set the cups down on the coffee table. She poured water from the little teapot into the tea cups. She picked her dolls up off the floor and sat them at the table.

"This is delicious," Johnny said as he drank his tea. Johnny pointed at the dolls. "And I like your little friends."

Connie didn't notice Johnny and Suzie's tea party. She and Eldridge were trying to figure out a problem on the computer.

"This is really delicious," Johnny said loudly. It was no good being nice to Connie's little sister if Connie didn't notice. Johnny drank a second cup of tea. "Suzie, thank you for the tea party with your dolls!"

Finally, Connie turned around.

"Oh no!" Connie yelled. "I should have been watching my sister."

"It's okay," Johnny said. "I'm happy to play with her."

"I hope you didn't drink the tea," Connie said.

"I had two cups already. And I played with her dolls. Because I'm nice," Johnny said and smiled.

"More tea please," Johnny said to Suzie.

"That's not a good idea," Connie said.

"What? It's not good to be nice?" Johnny asked.

"You don't understand," Connie said. "Suzie is little. She can't reach the taps on the sink."

"So?" Johnny asked.

"The only place Suzie can get water for her teapot is from the toilet," said Connie.

Chapter Three
Friends No More

"You should have been there this afternoon," Stu said to Tom. "When Connie told Johnny the water in her sister's teapot was from the toilet, Johnny ran straight to the bathroom. He should have closed the door. All of us heard him throw up."

"Is that true, Eldridge?" Tom asked.

Johnny, Stu, Tom and Eldridge skated out onto the Howling Timberwolves' end of the ice. At the other end, the Sharks, a team from a small town nearby, warmed up.

"It's true," Eldridge said. "Johnny threw up three times. Connie tried not to laugh, but she couldn't help it."

14

"Wow," Tom said to Johnny. "You really know how to get a girl's attention."

"Ha, ha," Johnny said. "Maybe tomorrow I should climb a flagpole and slide down as fast as I can."

"Ha, ha," Tom said. "What color was the water you drank from the teapot?"

Johnny and Tom started pushing each other.

"Hey," Stu said, "look!"

Connie walked into the rink with a couple of girls from their school.

Johnny and Tom stopped pushing each other to wave at Connie. She waved back.

"She came to watch me," Johnny said. "Today at school I told her about the game so she could see me play. That will make her want to be my dance partner. And then I'll win the hockey stick and all the other prizes."

"Not so fast," Tom said. "I told her about the game too. She's here to watch me. I'm the one who's going to the dance with her. She'll want to go with

15

me after she sees me play tonight. I'm going to beat you, Johnny, and win the dance contest."

The ref blew the whistle to start the game.

Eldridge and Stu skated off the ice to the players' box. Tom lined up at center for the face-off. Johnny was the right winger.

When the ref dropped the puck, Tom knocked it toward Johnny.

Tom shot forward and was open for a pass back from Johnny. But Johnny kept the puck. He stickhandled past the Sharks' winger. The Sharks' defenseman moved forward to block him. But Johnny poked the puck between the defenseman's skates and kept control of the puck.

Now it was two on one. Johnny and Tom against the other Sharks' defenseman.

"I'm open," Tom shouted. He broke hard for a pass.

But Johnny didn't pass. He fired a hard, fast shot. The puck went over the goalie's shoulders and into the upper right corner of the net.

Goal!

Johnny raised his arms and stick in the air. He turned in a wide circle toward the fans. He wanted to be sure Connie knew *he* had scored the goal.

Suddenly, he skated over a hockey stick and tripped. He fell forward onto his chest and slid into the boards. *Thump*!

The fans laughed.

Tom skated over to him. "Are you okay?" Tom asked. He helped Johnny up.

"Sure," Johnny said. "What happened?"

"I'm so sorry," Tom said. "You accidentally stepped on my stick."

"Accidentally!?" Johnny shouted. He pushed Tom. "You did that on purpose."

"I was wide open," Tom said. He pushed Johnny back. "You could have passed to me."

"But I scored," Johnny said. He shoved Tom again. "And you didn't. Plus you tripped me."

Tom shoved him back. The referee skated over and stepped between them. He stayed between them as they skated toward the players' bench.

"That's it!" Coach Smith yelled. "You two aren't playing until the third period!"

Stu and Eldridge skated onto the ice. They would get a lot more playing time now that Johnny and Tom were benched.

Stu stopped in front of Johnny and Tom.

"Wow," Stu said, "you guys really know how to get a girl's attention."

Chapter Four
Another Kind of Contest

The next morning before school started, Johnny saw Eldridge and Connie sitting together at a table in the library.

"Hey, guys," Johnny said.

"Hey," Eldridge said.

"Hey," Connie said.

"What's up?" Johnny asked. He didn't really care. He just wanted to talk to Connie. He hoped she would mention the goal he scored the night before.

"I'm trying get caught up on my homework," Connie said. Several books lay open on the table.

"When you start at a new school, you start off behind. Eldridge is a big help."

Johnny waited for her to say something about the goal. She looked back down at her books instead.

"Did you see my goal last night?" Johnny asked.

"Tom scored a great goal too," Eldridge said. "Good thing Coach Smith let you both back on the ice early."

"Hey, guys," another voice said. It was Tom. "What's up?"

Johnny turned around.

"What's up?" Johnny said. "Just helping Connie with her homework."

"She would be smarter to let Eldridge help her," Tom said. "Not a dummy like you."

"Maybe you should go back outside and climb a flagpole," Johnny said.

"And maybe you should drink some more toilet water," Tom said.

Johnny and Tom glared at each other.

"This is what I think of you," Johnny said. He put his left hand under his shirt and stuck it in his armpit. He flapped his right arm like a chicken wing. It made a loud rude noise.

Connie and Eldridge giggled.

"Is that the best you can do?" Tom said. "Listen to this one." Tom made an armpit noise too. It was even louder than Johnny's.

"Ha," Johnny said. "Well, I can do it behind my knee." He proved it by pulling his pant leg up. He put his hand behind his knee. He squeezed his leg against his hand. It made a loud sound.

Tom answered by making three quick noises under his armpit.

Johnny was not going to let Tom win. He put his hand back under his shirt and did four more noises. Four very, very loud noises.

But they were not as loud as the voice that came from behind a bookshelf.

"What is going on here?" the loud voice said. It was Mr. Wright. He stepped out from behind the shelf.

Mr. Wright was the school principal. He did not look happy. That was often the case when he saw Johnny or Tom. They had been in his office before. There was a sign on his desk that said *The name is Mr. Wright, never Mr. Wrong. And don't forget it.*

"What's going on here?" Mr. Wright asked again.

Johnny thought that wasn't a smart question. Anyone who could hear knew the answer. Mr. Wright could hear. So why was he asking?

"Tom was making trumpet noises," Johnny explained, "with his armpit. He's very good at it."

"So was Johnny," Tom said quickly. "He's even better at it. His were louder. And he wasn't trying to sound like a trumpet. He was trying to sound like a—"

"Enough!" Mr. Wright said. "Somehow I don't think it matters who made the loudest trumpet noises."

"Oh, that's good," Johnny said. "For a second, I thought you would be mad at us and want to have another special talk."

Mr. Wright sighed. "Come with me," he said. "I think both of you know the way to my office."

Chapter Five
What Does a Car Taste Like?

The next morning before the bell rang, Tom saw Johnny and Stu standing beside a car in the school parking lot. Their backpacks lay on the ground in front of them.

"Hey, Tom," Stu said. "Johnny is a big fat chicken."

Johnny shook his head. "I am not."

"You are too," Stu said. "I even double-dog dared you, and you wouldn't do it."

Johnny shook his head again. "I am not."

"Why is he a big fat chicken?" Tom asked. "What did you double-dog dare him to do?"

"I double-dog dared him to lick the bumper of this old car," Stu said. Stu pointed at the car beside them.

"That doesn't make him a chicken," Tom said. "That makes him smart. Everybody knows on a cold day like this your tongue would freeze to the bumper."

"No," Stu said, "it won't."

"I remember a kid who licked the flagpole," Tom said. "He was stuck there for a long time."

"That's a flagpole," Stu explained. "Flagpoles don't have chrome."

Stu pointed at the bumper. It was shiny and made of chrome.

"Magnets stick to flagpoles," Stu said. "Magnets don't stick to chrome. Chrome is different," Stu explained. "A person's tongue won't stick to chrome."

"Really?" Tom asked.

"Sure," Stu said. "Watch this."

Stu got on his hands and knees. He leaned forward and licked the chrome bumper. His tongue did not stick. Stu got up again. "See?"

Tom laughed. "I guess that does make Johnny a big fat chicken."

"You do it then, Tom," Johnny said. "I dare you. No, I double-dog dare you."

"You shouldn't have said that," Stu told Johnny. "Now Tom's going to do it, and Connie will hear that you chickened out."

"Okay, Tom," Johnny said, "I take back the double-dog dare."

"Too late," Tom said. "When Connie hears you're a big fat chicken, she'll decide to go to the dance with me."

Tom got on his hands and knees and crawled toward the bumper. He leaned his head forward. He stuck his tongue out and licked the bumper.

Tom's tongue instantly froze to the bumper.

"Aaaaack!" Tom said.

"Don't yank your tongue loose," Johnny said. "You'll rip the skin off. I saw a little kid do that once after he was stupid enough to lick a flagpole."

"Aaaaack!" Tom said. Then he said something that sounded like "help." It was hard to understand him. Most of his tongue was stuck to the bumper.

"I think he's saying 'help,'" Johnny said. "Just wait. I have something in my backpack that might be helpful."

Johnny kneeled beside his backpack and opened it. He pulled out a camera and started taking photos of Tom with his tongue stuck to the bumper.

"Aaaaaack!" Tom said.

"I agree," Johnny said. "You do look silly. And when Connie sees these photos, she'll know I'm the one she should dance with at the Valentine's fundraiser."

"Aaaaaack!" Tom said.

"What's that?" Johnny asked. "How come Stu's tongue didn't stick to the bumper?"

31

Johnny pulled out a tube of Vaseline. "This stuff is greasy and it doesn't freeze. We put it on the part of the bumper that Stu licked. His tongue just slid off the grease."

Johnny took a bunch of photos of Tom on his hands and knees with his tongue stuck to the bumper of the car.

"Aaaaaack!" Tom said.

"It's hard to understand you," Johnny said. "But I think you want help, right?"

"Uh-huh," Tom said, on his hands and knees. "Uh-huh. Uh-huh. Uh-huh."

"Okay," Johnny answered. "We'll go into the school and ask a teacher to come and pour warm water over your tongue. Then you'll be unstuck."

Johnny looked at Stu. "We should ask Mr. Wright, shouldn't we? Isn't this his car?"

Chapter Six
A Divided Twosome

That night, the Howling Timberwolves played another home game. This time they faced the Pirates from out of town. The Timberwolves had not lost to the Pirates all season.

"Easy game tonight," Johnny said to Tom as they skated during the pregame warm-ups.

Tom didn't answer.

"Are you're still mad at me for this morning?" Johnny asked. He waved at Connie, who was sitting in the stands. "It was a joke. If you and I had tricked Stu into licking a car bumper, you'd still be laughing."

Connie waved back. Tom did not look at Connie.

"I don't want to play on your line tonight," Tom said.

"I guess you're still mad at me."

"Coach Smith said I could try playing on the line with Eldridge," Tom said.

"But the team needs us to play together," Johnny said. "We're the line that scores the goals. We need Eldridge and his line to stop the other team from scoring. They are the defensive line. That's how we win."

"I don't want to play on your line," Tom said.

"Come on," Johnny said. "It was a little joke. It's not like the whole world knows about it."

They stopped talking for a second as a defenseman for the Pirates skated over to them.

"Hey," the defenseman said, "I heard some idiot on your team licked a car today and froze his tongue to the bumper. Is that true?"

"Wow," Johnny said, "news travels fast."

"It should," the defenseman said to Johnny. "You're the one who told my teammate about it."

The defenseman skated away.

"Like I said," Tom told Johnny, "I would rather play on the line with Eldridge."

Tom skated over to the bench.

He didn't play a shift with Johnny the whole night.

And the Timberwolves lost 9–5 to the Pirates.

Chapter Seven
Who Looks Worse?

"This will be an easy test," Tom told Johnny. "And the best way to get a girl's attention."

They were in the school gym at the end of lunch hour. Stu was there too. Stu had a video camera.

"What's the test?" Johnny asked.

"When Connie sees who has the biggest muscles," Tom said, "she'll know who's the strongest and who she should go to the dance with."

"Not a bad idea," Johnny said. "Maybe that will make up for watching us lose last night's game. How does your contest work?"

Tom pointed at the gymnastic rings hanging from the ceiling.

"I'm going to take my shirt off, grab on to those rings and pull myself up. You'll be able to see my giant muscles. And Stu will video how long I can stay up there," Tom explained. "Then it's your turn, and Stu will video you too. There's no way you'll be able to hold yourself up longer than I can."

"Okay, but I'm not going to like making you look bad two days in a row," Johnny said. "When Connie goes to the dance with me, just remember this was your idea."

"Ha!" Tom said. He took off his shirt. He posed for the video camera. He flexed his muscles. Then he jumped up, grabbed the wooden rings and pulled himself up with a mighty grunt. He stayed there for ninety seconds. Finally, he was so tired he dropped to the ground.

"Look at the clock," Tom said, pointing at the big white clock on the gym wall. "There is no way you're going to last longer than ninety seconds."

"Impressive," Johnny said. "But not as impressive as I will be. You guys are right. This is a great way to get a girl's attention."

Johnny took off his shirt. He flexed his muscles. He jumped up and grabbed the rings. He pulled himself up with a mighty grunt. As he held himself up, he stared at the clock. He counted the seconds. There was no way he was going to let Tom win this contest. Especially with Stu recording it.

Johnny heard a chair scrape against the floor behind him. Then he felt something cold on his back that pushed him forward.

"Hey!" Johnny said. But he didn't let go. He was only at seventy seconds. He needed to hang on for at least ninety-one seconds to win.

The cold thing on his back pushed against him even harder. Johnny couldn't see it.

"I know that's you, Tom," Johnny said. "You're trying to make me lose. But it won't work."

The thing on his back felt hard and round, but it didn't hurt. Johnny gripped the rings tightly. When the cold round thing stopped pushing him forward, Johnny swung backward. Something was still stuck to his back.

Tom appeared in front of Johnny and waved.

Johnny didn't care what was stuck to his back. Tom wasn't going to trick him into letting go.

Johnny stared hard at the clock. His arms were tired. He only had to hold on for another ten seconds to beat Tom.

Stu moved to the side and kept filming Johnny.

"I'm going to win," Johnny said loudly to the camera. He watched the clock. To beat Tom, all he had to do was stay up for six more seconds.

Five…Four…Three…Two…One…

"I win!" Johnny shouted. He dropped down from the rings. He raised his arms in triumph and posed for the video camera.

"Nice try, Tom," Johnny said. "But your dirty trick didn't work."

Now Johnny could finally take off the thing stuck on his back.

He reached behind himself. His hands touched a wooden handle. The handle stuck straight out of his back. It was as if he had been shot by a giant arrow. But it didn't hurt.

He yanked at the handle. The round thing on his back pulled at his skin.

What was going on? What was on his back?

He had to reach so far behind himself it was hard to get a good grip on the handle.

He tried tugging the stick from side to side. But the round thing remained stuck to his back and pulled on his skin.

"Are you getting this on video?" Tom asked Stu. "It should look much better than the photos Johnny took of me yesterday. Connie will think this is very funny."

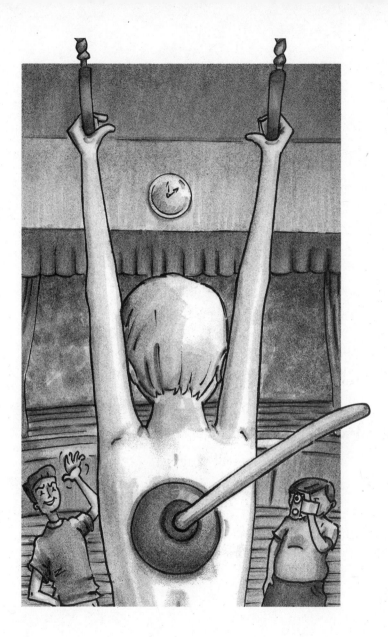

"What's going on?" Johnny asked.

"I pushed a toilet-bowl plunger onto your back," Tom said. "I don't think Connie will want to dance with someone who runs around the gym with a plunger stuck to him."

"This isn't funny!" Johnny said.

"Sure it is," Tom said. "If you and I had done this to Stu, you'd be laughing."

"Come on," Johnny said. "Help me."

Tom took Johnny's shirt and ran out of the gym. Stu followed.

Johnny couldn't leave the gym without the whole school seeing him. He was trapped. His shirt was off. And he had a plunger stuck to his back.

That's when the bell rang.

And all the girls came in for dance class.

Chapter Eight
The Truth Comes Out

At school the next morning, Johnny walked down the hall toward his classroom. Through a window of the library, he saw something that made him stop.

He quickly stepped away from the window and flattened himself against the wall.

He peeked around the corner to look in the window again.

And then he ran out to the playground to find Tom.

"Come inside," Johnny said. "Quick."

"I'm not falling for that," Tom said.

"Falling for what?"

"You're going to play a trick on me. To get me back for the toilet plunger on your back. Which I only did to get back at you for making me lick a bumper."

"Was it your idea to put the toilet plunger on my back?" Johnny asked. "Or was it Stu's idea?"

"Stu's. He said it would make you look bad when Connie saw the video."

"Guess what," Johnny said. "It was Stu's idea to get you to stick your tongue on the bumper. He said it would make *you* look bad when Connie saw the photos."

"Why would he want both of us to look bad?" Tom asked.

"I should have known." Johnny shook his head in disgust. "Two words: *free dinner*."

Tom understood immediately. "Stu wants Connie to be his dance partner so he can win the free dinners."

"Guess what else," Johnny said. "Right now Stu's in the library with Connie, helping her with her

47

homework. While we look bad, he's making himself look good."

"That rat," Tom said. "That dog. Making the two of us fight over a girl. It got us in trouble. It made us lose a hockey game. What are we going to do?"

"Whatever it is," Johnny said, "he's going to wish he hadn't messed with us."

Chapter Nine
Stu Wants a Milkshake

Ting!

"Ha," Tom said, "that's four in a row. One more and I win."

Tom and Johnny were in the science room during a break between classes. They stood at the back of the room next to a table with a glass of water on it. Tom had a metal funnel tucked into the front of his pants.

"Hey," Stu said when he walked in for science class. "What's the game?"

"Watch," Johnny said.

Tom took a penny out of the funnel and leaned his head back. He placed the penny on his chin.

Then he dropped his chin. The penny slid off his chin and straight down.

Ting! The penny landed in the funnel.

"Five in a row," Tom said. "Johnny, now you owe me a milkshake."

"A milkshake?" Stu said. "A milkshake?"

More students walked into the classroom.

"Yeah," Tom said, "a large chocolate milkshake."

"Can I try?" Stu said. "I'd love to win a milkshake."

"Okay, but if you don't get at least five in a row," Johnny said, "you have to buy Tom a milkshake."

"I won't lose," Stu said. "Not when it comes to food. I'll do almost anything for food."

Stu grabbed the funnel. He tucked the bottom of the funnel into the front of his pants.

"Give me the penny," Stu said. "Hurry. Before the rest of the class gets here."

Stu leaned his head back. He put the penny on his chin. He dropped his chin. The penny slid off his chin and straight down.

Ting!

"Ha," Stu said. "That's one. You don't mess with me when it comes to free food."

"I guess not," Johnny said. "You'll do almost anything for food."

"Johnny's right about that," Tom said.

Stu grabbed the penny again. He leaned his head back. As he put the penny on his chin, he didn't see Tom grab the glass of water off the table. Tom hid the glass behind his back.

Stu dropped his chin. The penny slid down into the funnel.

Ting!

Stu was in a hurry to win before the teacher came into the room. He grabbed the penny from the funnel. He leaned his head back. He put the penny on his chin.

While he was looking up at the ceiling, Tom poured the glass of water into the funnel. All the water ran into Stu's pants.

"Aaaaack!" Stu said. He jerked his head. The penny fell to the floor. Johnny grabbed the funnel and pulled it out of Stu's pants. He put the funnel back with the rest of the science equipment. Tom put the glass back on the table.

"Aaaack!" Stu said. He looked down at his pants. The water had soaked through the front of his pants. It looked like he had wet himself.

That's when Connie walked into the room with Eldridge.

Chapter Ten
The Best Man Wins

"Okay, okay, okay," Stu said. "I was wrong. I admit it. I should never have made you two play tricks on each other to look bad in front of Connie. But I want to take Connie to the dance for the free dinners. How's that different from you two?"

It was lunch hour. Stu and Johnny and Tom sat together at a table in the cafeteria.

"That's true," Johnny said. "I want the graphite hockey stick."

"And I just enjoy winning, especially if Johnny loses," Tom said. "I guess we shouldn't get mad at each other over this."

"Are you going to finish that?" Stu pointed at the last half of Johnny's hamburger.

"No," Johnny said.

Stu put the leftover hamburger in his mouth. He chewed twice and swallowed.

"Even if we aren't mad at each other, we have a problem," Johnny said. "There are three of us. Connie can only go to the dance with one of us."

"It's not a problem," Tom said. "I say let the best man win. Let's see who really got her attention."

"That might not be the real problem," Stu said. "Has it occurred to either of you that we actually have to ask Connie to go to the dance, not just get her attention?"

"Oh," Johnny said.

"Oh," Tom said.

The three friends thought about this in silence for about a minute.

"She's probably in the library," Stu said. He stood up. "Eldridge has been helping her with math."

Tom stood up. "It would be easier to ask her if we were together."

Johnny stood up. "I'm not scared to ask her, but I'll come with you to help you guys out."

They found Connie and Eldridge at a table in the library with their books open.

"You first," Johnny said to Tom.

"No, you first," Tom said to Johnny.

Both of them looked at Stu. "You first."

That didn't work.

"Rock, paper, scissors," Johnny said. "Loser goes first."

They played rock, paper, scissors.

Tom lost, and then Stu lost. Johnny was going to be the last one to ask her.

Tom said, "Connie, you're a good dancer. Will you go to the Valentine's fundraiser with me?"

"I'm sorry," Connie said. "I would like to, but not this time."

Stu said, "Connie, I would like to win the free dinners. Will you go to the Valentine's fundraiser with me?"

"I'm sorry," Connie said. "I would like to, but not this time."

"Like you said," Johnny told Tom, "may the best man win."

Johnny said, "Connie, don't think I'm asking because I think you are cute or anything like that, but will you go to the Valentine's fundraiser with me?"

"I'm sorry," Connie said. "I would like to, but not this time."

"Is it because I hurt myself on the flagpole and licked a bumper?" Tom said.

"No," Connie said, "I thought that was funny."

"Is it because it looked like I wet my pants in science class?" Stu said.

"No," Connie said, "I thought that was funny."

"Is it because I drank toilet water and had a plunger stuck to my back?" Johnny said.

"No," Connie said, "I thought that was funny too."

"Then why not?" Tom asked. "How could you say no to all of us?"

"Because I want to go with Eldridge," Connie answered.

"Eldridge?" Johnny said. "He didn't even score any goals for the Timberwolves."

"Eldridge?" Tom said. "He can't even make a good armpit noise."

"Eldridge?" Stu said. "What did he do?"

"Me?" Eldridge said. "I never thought about going to the dance. I'm too shy."

"You've spent a lot of time helping me with my computer and my homework," Connie said to Eldridge. "Once I heard about the Valentine's fundraiser, I thought it might be nice to help you too. I'm a pretty good dancer, so there's a good chance we might win the dance contest. Do you think you'd like to go with me?"

"Sure," Eldridge said, "as long as you'll teach me to dance."

Johnny, Tom and Stu turned to leave.

As they walked out of the library, Johnny shook his head at Tom and Stu and said, "Girls! I don't know if I'll ever understand them."

Sigmund Brouwer is the best-selling author of many books for children and young adults. Sigmund loves visiting schools and talking to children about reading and writing. *Timberwolf Rivals* is his seventh book about the Timberwolves. The other books in the series include *Timberwolf Challenge*, *Timberwolf Chase*, *Timberwolf Hunt*, *Timberwolf Revenge*, *Timberwolf Trap* and *Timberwolf Tracks*.